STAR GOLD

Leo P. Kelley

A Pacemaker® Book

Fearon Education
a division of
David S. Lake Publishers
Belmont, California

The PACEMAKER BESTELLERS

Bestellers I

Diamonds in the Dirt
Night of the Kachina
The Verlaine Crossing
Silvabamba
The Money Game

Flight to Fear
The Time Trap
The Candy Man
Three Mile House
Dream of the Dead

Bestellers II

Black Beach
Crash Dive
Wind Over Stonehenge
Gypsy
Escape from Tomorrow

The Demeter Star
North to Oak Island
So Wild a Dream
Wet Fire
Tiger, Lion, Hawk

Bestellers III

Star Gold
Bad Moon
Jungle Jenny
Secret Spy
Little Big Top

The Animals
Counterfeit!
Night of Fire and Blood
Village of Vampires
I Died Here

Bestellers IV

Dares
Welcome to Skull Canyon
Blackbeard's Medal
Time's Reach
Trouble at Catskill Creek

The Cardiff Hill Mystery
Tomorrow's Child
Hong Kong Heat
Follow the Whales
A Changed Man

Series director: Robert G. Bander

Designer: Richard Kharibian

Cover designer and illustrator: Cliff Spohn

ISBN-0-8224-5369-X

Library of Congress Catalog Card Number: 78-72333

Printed in the United States of America.

10 9 8 7 6 5 4

CONTENTS

CHAPTER 1
THE PRISON PLANET

He was a big man. And a strong one.

His body was brown from the sun. His long, black hair covered his ears. His deep brown eyes missed nothing.

He had on torn shorts. No shirt. No shoes.

His name was Brett Kinkaid. Once he had killed a man.

That was why he had been put where he was —on Earth. On the prison planet that Earth had become more than 100 years ago, in the year 2041. Three years ago, in 2180, he had been put there for life.

He wondered—should he hide? No. It was too late to hide. They had seen him. Well, he thought, let them come. I'm ready for them. As ready as I'll ever be.

They were coming toward him now. Six of them. Six dirty, wild dogs. All of them hungry for meat—*any* kind of meat. Kinkaid felt his skin grow cold while a hot sun burned in the blue sky.

He could see their wet teeth shine. He heard them begin to bark.

The leader of the dog pack was black. He was the biggest of them all. Kinkaid had met the leader before. He called him Cyclops. Cyclops had two torn ears—thanks to Kinkaid—and one blind eye.

The dogs began to run toward him, barking. Their teeth—forget their teeth, Kinkaid thought to himself. He picked up a stone. He lifted his hand, and the stone flew from it.

The stone hit an ugly yellow dog on the side of its head. The dog dropped. Good, Kinkaid thought. One down and five to go.

And then the dogs were upon him.

He felt their stiff fur against his skin. Cyclops's teeth bit both of his hands. He let out a loud yell and grabbed Cyclops around the neck. He lifted the dog high above him. He threw Cyclops into the pack.

Then Kinkaid was in the dog pack. Kicking. Hitting.

He picked up one dog. It bit his face. Kinkaid

threw it against a tree. The dog didn't get up again. Then Kinkaid smashed Cyclops's head with a stick. Cyclops stopped moving. The other dogs turned tail and ran away.

Kinkaid pulled up some grass. He used it to wipe the blood from his face and hands. Then he walked on.

He walked past dead and broken trees.

Through a small town that was full of burned-out buildings. He tried not to think about the things he saw—all the dead things.

Once Earth had been beautiful. But that was before Earth's people had spoiled their own air and water. That was before their last war had turned Earth into a dead planet.

Now the planet was good for nothing. Nothing, that is, but a prison for criminals from many worlds.

The people of Earth had left their dead home. They had gone out to the stars. Now only criminals were sent to Earth to live as best they could. Or to die.

Kinkaid looked up at the sky. No spaceship was in sight. But soon one would come. It was time. Once every few weeks, a ship dropped food on the prison planet for the criminals. Kinkaid was on his way to make sure that he got some of that food.

But when he reached the place where the ship always dropped the food, he stopped. Other people were already there. They had beat him to it. He would probably have to fight for his food. Well, he *would* fight.

Then he saw her. She was with the other people. Karen. Karen of the beautiful eyes.

Karen who never laughed. Karen who always carried a knife—and could use it.

She saw him. But she didn't move or say anything.

He went up to her. "The ship's late," he said.

"Since when do you own a watch that works?" she said.

"It was just something to say." He looked up at the sky. And then at Karen again. He found it hard to believe that she was a criminal. But she was. She had told him what she had done. She had kidnapped a child to get money—lots of it. But the Space Police had caught her. And now she was here. And now she never laughed. Or even smiled.

The sound of a ship's jets filled the air.

Everyone looked up at the sky. The ship flew over. Then it circled and came back. A door opened in the side of the ship. Boxes and bags of food fell out. They crashed on the ground.

Kinkaid was the first person to reach the food. He kicked several boxes out of the pile. Then he stood over them. He didn't say anything. He just stood there.

A man started toward him, his hands reaching out, his eyes on the food.

"Mine," Kinkaid said.

"Oh, you think so?" said the man. Then he looked into Kinkaid's eyes. He backed away.

Kinkaid picked up all the food he could carry. He started back the way he had come. On the way, he passed Karen.

"Get much?" he asked her.

"Enough," was her answer.

Kinkaid saw the blood on her knife. "See you around," he said.

Karen said nothing.

When Kinkaid got home, Lor'l was waiting for him. The alien's one great eye grew large when he saw Kinkaid. The fur on his body changed from blue to green. Kinkaid knew from these signs that Lor'l was glad to see him.

Lor'l helped Kinkaid carry the boxes of food into their cave. The cave was in the side of a small hill.

"I saw no one while you were gone," Lor'l said. "I think we are safe in this new place of ours."

"Don't be too sure," Kinkaid said. "Keep your eyes—I mean, your eye—open."

"I have this," Lor'l said. He held a laser gun in one of his three-fingered hands.

"I know you do," Kinkaid said. "But a laser

gun isn't a sure thing against some of the people here."

Lor'l put the food away in the back of the cave. Then he started a fire.

As Kinkaid watched the alien, he had a thought. *This alien is the only real friend I have here.*

He thought about what Lor'l had told him a long time ago. Lor'l had taken some money that didn't belong to him. It hadn't been much money. But because of it he had been sent here to the prison planet.

Kinkaid began to cook some food over the fire Lor'l had made.

"You go," Lor'l said to him. "Swim. Have some fun."

Kinkaid went down to the river at the bottom of the hill. He took off his shorts. He jumped into the river and began to swim.

Soon he forgot all about meeting Cyclops and the pack of wild dogs. For a minute he even forgot where he was. And why.

But then Lor'l called his name. Then he remembered.

He climbed out of the river and let the sun dry his body. Then he put on his shorts.

He returned to the cave and ate what Lor'l had cooked. It didn't taste very good. But not because of the way Lor'l cooked it. Criminals didn't get very good food. Good food cost a lot of money.

"Thanks," Kinkaid said to Lor'l. "This is good," he lied.

Lor'l looked up at him. His eye closed, then opened. "You brought this food. Thanks to you."

Night came. Stars filled the sky.

Kinkaid lay down on the warm ground and

looked up at the stars. Beautiful, he thought. He thought about how good his life used to be. Once he had been up there with the stars. Then he had been Commander Kinkaid of the Space Police. His spaceship had been—. He closed his eyes.

"I see a ship," Lor'l said a few minutes later.

Kinkaid, lost in his thoughts of the past, didn't hear him.

"It is not a prison ship," Lor'l said.

Kinkaid opened his eyes and sat up. He couldn't see any ship in the dark. But then he heard its loud jets.

"Now there are two ships," Lor'l said. "The second one is a Space Police ship."

Kinkaid watched the sky. Soon he could see the lights of the two ships. The ships came closer. Then the Space Police drove the other ship away.

Kinkaid thought about what had just happened. It had happened before. Sometimes ships came close to the prison planet. The people on them wanted to see what life was like for the criminals. Sometimes they even tried to land to get a better look. But the Space Police always drove them away. If a ship landed, some of the criminals might try to escape in it. It was one of the jobs of the Space Police to see that that didn't happen.

Hours later, Kinkaid went to sleep.

Almost at once, Lor'l woke him. "A woman has come. She would speak with you."

"Now?" an angry Kinkaid yelled. "At this time of night? Tell her to go away and come back in the morning."

Karen came into the cave. "Shut up, Kinkaid, and listen to me."

He listened. But he couldn't believe what Karen said. She told him that a ship had just landed. The ship belonged to Adam Lane. Kinkaid had heard of Adam Lane. Lane was a very rich man. He was in business on all the worlds there were. And Karen said that Lane wanted to talk to Kinkaid right away.

CHAPTER **2**

TAKE IT OR LEAVE IT

"What does he want to talk to me about?" Kinkaid asked Karen.

"He didn't tell me. He just asked if anyone knew where you were. I said I did. He gave me some food to come here and tell you he wants to talk to you. Now I've done my job. Good-bye."

"Wait a minute," Kinkaid said. "Where is Lane?"

"I can show you," Karen said. "What will you give me to show you?"

"No food."

"Wait," Lor'l said. "I will get something." He went to the back of the cave. When he returned, he gave Karen some animal skins.

"Come on," she said to Kinkaid. "I'll take you to Lane."

"Do you want me to come with you, Kinkaid?" Lor'l asked.

"No. Stay here, Lor'l. Don't let anyone near the cave."

Lor'l picked up his laser gun.

Kinkaid followed Karen out of the cave. They moved through the dark night. As he walked, Kinkaid wondered why Lane wanted to talk to him.

He was still wondering when they reached Lane's ship. The crew of the ship had covered it with a net. They had placed grass and dirt on the net so the ship couldn't be seen from the sky.

A lot of people stood near the ship. Karen spoke to some of them, and then left.

Kinkaid went up to the ship. "Lane!" he yelled.

A door opened in the side of the ship. A fat man came through the door and down the steps. He was a small, round ball of a man. He was almost too fat to walk. He had no hair on his head.

"You're Adam Lane?" Kinkaid said to him.

"I am. And you're Brett Kinkaid. I remember you from your pictures in the papers. But you've changed, Kinkaid."

"This place changes a person."

"Yes, I suppose it would." Lane looked around him. It was easy to tell that he didn't like what he saw.

The crowd of people moved closer to the ship. Lane barked orders at his crew. The crew took out their laser guns. They fired at the ground in front of the people. The people turned and ran away.

"Now then—to business," Lane said. "I—"

"I want to ask you something first," Kinkaid said. "Was it your ship that the Space Police drove away before?"

Lane smiled and said, "Yes, it was. But I came back, as you can see. I waited for the police to leave. Then I returned."

Kinkaid looked at the ship under the net.

And then at Lane. He waited for the man to speak.

"You've been here for two years now, haven't you?"

"Three," Kinkaid said.

"Well, Kinkaid, you never should have killed that man on your spaceship."

"I killed him in self-defense. He started the fight. He tried to kill me."

"That's not what his friend from the ship said at your trial. He said you killed his friend for no reason at all."

"That's not true. The man lied. The man I shot was a crooked cop. He felt passed over. He wanted my job. That's why he tried to kill me. He wanted me out of the way so he could run the show. Then his friend lied at my trial about what happened. And I was sent here."

"Well, never mind about that now," Lane said. "All that's in the past. I'm interested in the present. And in you, Kinkaid."

"Why?"

"Because my daughter—her name is Alison—has been kidnapped. I want you to get her back."

"Who kidnapped her?"

"The Albans. They are holding her on their star—on Alba."

"I've never heard of that star."

"That's because you've been out of touch, Kinkaid. Alba was just found a year ago. *I* found it. A dead star. I set up a small human colony there. Alison lives there with me. But now the alien Albans are killing our people there. And they've kidnapped Alison. They say they will let her go if my people and I leave Alba. Well, we won't leave."

"Why don't you go to the Space Police?"

"The Albans said they would kill Alison if I did. If Space Police ships showed up there— well, you can see my problem. So I came to you. You were the best commander the Space Police ever had. You were young for the job, but good at it. If anyone can save Alison, you can."

"What do I get out of this if I help you?"

"Good question," Lane said with a smile. "Yes, a very good question. Kinkaid, I can get you out of here for good. I have friends who have power. They will speak to the right people. Then those people will sign the right papers. And you, Kinkaid, will be a free man for good."

"You know, of course, that it's against the

law to help anyone at all escape from here?"

Lane waved a hand. "You want to get out of here, don't you? Am I right about that?"

"Yes, I want to get out of here," Kinkaid said.

"I thought you might be sick of leading a pig's life by now," Lane said.

Kinkaid was. He thought about good food. He thought about clean clothes. He thought about being able to live as a free man once more.

"Then you'll do it?" Lane asked. "You'll get Alison back for me?"

Kinkaid turned away. He thought of Cyclops and the other wild dogs. He had killed Cyclops. But other dogs would take his place. He thought about fighting people to get enough to eat.

And he thought about getting old. Too old to fight. Then, he thought, the dogs will win. Someone faster and stronger will always get to the food first.

He turned back to Lane. The fat, little man still smiled at him. Kinkaid's teeth ground together.

"I'll need a spaceship," Kinkaid said. "And a crew."

"You can take my ship," Lane said. "You can drop me off at Moon Base Two and then go on to Alba. But you'll have to find your own crew. Perhaps some of your friends here?"

Lor'l, Kinkaid thought. And then—*Karen*. She wasn't a good friend like Lor'l was. But she was very good in a fight.

"I'll find a crew," Kinkaid told Lane.

"Good."

"One more thing," Kinkaid said. "I want the ones I pick for my crew to go free once this is all over."

Lane stopped smiling. "That won't be so easy to fix."

"That's the deal," Kinkaid said. "Take it or leave it."

Lane's smile returned. "I'll take it. Pick your crew. Be ready to leave with me on my ship first thing in the morning."

Lane climbed the steps to his ship. He went into it, and the door closed behind him.

Kinkaid turned and ran. When he was near the cave, he let out a yell. Lor'l, laser gun in hand, came out of the cave.

"It's me," Kinkaid said. "I've got some good news for you, old friend."

He told Lor'l about Lane and about what Lane had said. "So that's the deal," he said. "Do you want to come with me, Lor'l?"

Lor'l's fur changed from blue to green. "It will be good to be free again. I have a family at home. It will be good to see them again. I never thought I would."

Kinkaid held out his hand. Lor'l shook it.

Then Kinkaid said, "It looks like I'm not going to get any sleep tonight. I've got too much to do. Wait here for me, Lor'l. I'll be back soon."

And then he was gone, running through the night. He was happy. As he ran, he looked up at the stars. Soon he would escape to them. He spoke to them in a very soft voice.

"Wait for me," he said. "I'm coming. I'm coming back to you."

CHAPTER **3**

TO THE STAR ALBA

It took Kinkaid some time to find Karen. When he did, he saw that she was sleeping. He reached down and touched her arm.

She was on her feet at once. In her hand was a knife. She used it on Kinkaid. He let out a yell and jumped back. Then he grabbed his hand where she had cut it.

"It's me—Kinkaid!" he yelled at her. "Put that knife away!" He felt the warm blood on his hand where Karen's knife had cut him.

"What do you want?" she asked. She didn't put the knife away.

"I came to make a deal with you," Kinkaid said.

"Oh? Since when do you make deals, Kinkaid? I thought you were interested in only one person—Brett Kinkaid."

"Listen to me." Kinkaid told her about the

deal he had worked out with Lane. Then he said, "Just think of it, Karen. We can get away from here. We can be free again."

"Free," Karen said, as if she were tasting the word. She looked around her and then at Kinkaid. "I'll join your crew," she said.

"Good. Lor'l will be with us too."

"Lor'l? What do you want him for? He's an alien—an animal."

"He isn't an animal. Besides, he's my friend."

"You sure do have strange friends," Karen said.

"I'll need one more person in the crew. I don't know who."

"Zeno," Karen said.

Kinkaid knew Zeno. But not very well. He knew that Zeno's father had been human. But Zeno's mother had been an alien. Zeno looked almost human. But he had pink eyes and green hair. And long teeth that were as sharp as any rat's.

"He's good with a gun," Karen said.

"Where is he? Do you know?"

Karen led him to a tree. Zeno spent his nights in the branches. She called his name.

Zeno woke up and looked down at them.

"Kinkaid wants to talk to you," Karen called up to him. "Come down here."

Zeno climbed down from the tree.

Kinkaid told him about the deal he had made with Lane.

Zeno said, "It should be easy to get Lane's daughter back. All we have to do is wipe out the Albans."

"Don't be too sure," Kinkaid said. "Lane told me that the Albans have killed some of the humans on their star. They just might do the same to us."

"When do we leave?" Zeno asked. "And how?"

"In the morning," Kinkaid answered. "On Lane's ship." He looked up at the sky. "It's almost morning already. Let's head for the ship."

They did. On the way, they picked up Lor'l. When the sun came up, it found them standing outside Lane's ship. It wasn't long before Lane came out of it.

"We're ready to leave," Kinkaid told him.

"So am I," Lane said. "Get on board."

Kinkaid and the others did as they were told. Outside, the crew took the net off the ship. Then they got on board. And Lane gave the order to leave the prison planet.

Just then, one of the crew said, "Here comes real trouble."

In the sky above them was a Space Police ship.

Lane ordered his crew to take the ship up. Once in the sky, he said, "Get to the guns."

Three of the crew raced to the gun stations.

"Fire!" Lane ordered.

Red light streamed from the guns. The red light hit the Space Police ship. The crew on the ship fired back. But they were no match for Lane's ship. Minutes later, the police ship lost power and began to fall.

Watching through a window, Kinkaid saw the ship hit the ground. It turned into a big ball of fire.

He closed his eyes. Maybe someone I once knew was on that ship, he thought. Maybe someone from my old command was on board. He forced himself to think of other things—of the job he had to do on Alba.

Lane's ship landed at Moon Base Two some time later. There Kinkaid and his crew changed into clothes Lane gave them. They ate. While they were eating, Lane left.

When he was gone, Karen spoke to Kinkaid.

"We could take this ship. We could go where we want."

Zeno said, "That's a good idea. Let's forget about Lane's daughter. Let's just take off."

Zeno stopped talking as Lane came into the room. "I heard what you just said. Yes, you could just forget about Alison. But I don't think that would be a good idea. My men would hunt you down. They would find you, be sure of it. And when they did, they would kill you."

No one spoke.

Lane said, "I'm leaving the ship now. I'll wait here at Moon Base Two. When you get Alison away from the Albans, bring her here. And remember what I just told you about my men. They enjoy a good hunt."

When Lane was gone, Kinkaid got ready to leave Moon Base Two. It felt good to touch the controls of a ship again. It seemed to him that the three years he had spent on the prison planet had been a dream–a bad dream. Now he was back where he belonged. Once again he was doing what he believed he had been born to do. He pressed several buttons. Then he set the ship's course for Alba. He showed Karen how to control the ship.

Several hours later, she took control of the ship so Kinkaid could get some sleep. Lor'l asked her if she wanted him to help her. She sent him away. Zeno walked about the ship touching all the guns.

It took them a long time to reach Alba. But at last they did. Kinkaid returned to the controls. As he was about to bring the ship down on the star, an Alban ship flew toward them. The ship sent a message to Kinkaid.

"Are you humans?" a voice from the Alban ship asked.

"Yes," Kinkaid answered.

"Go away," the Alban said. "We want no more humans here."

But Kinkaid kept on his course. Then the Alban ship fired and hit Kinkaid's ship. It rocked from side to side.

"Return their fire!" Kinkaid ordered.

Zeno let out a happy yell. He got behind one of the laser guns and fired twice. Red flashes of light flew from his gun. One of them hit the Alban ship. "*Got it!*" Zeno yelled. He fired several more times.

The Alban ship blew up.

"That's enough, Zeno," Kinkaid said.

But Zeno kept shooting at pieces of the Alban ship.

"Cut it out!" Kinkaid yelled. "Don't waste our fire power. We may need it later."

When Zeno kept on firing, Kinkaid ran over to him. He pulled him away from the gun.

Zeno hit Kinkaid.

Kinkaid hit him back—two hard punches. Zeno fell to the floor.

Zeno looked up at him. He showed his sharp teeth. "You'll pay for this, Kinkaid," he said.

Kinkaid left him on the floor and returned

to the control board. He got ready to land. Just then another Alban ship came after them.

"Take control of the ship," Kinkaid ordered Karen. He went to one of the laser guns. "Zeno, get on the other gun."

Zeno didn't move.

Kinkaid called to Lor'l. Both of them began to fire. Lor'l brought the Alban ship down.

"We can land now," Kinkaid told Karen.

She brought the ship down on the star.

CHAPTER **4**
Good-bye, Lor'l

When the ship landed, Karen cut its jets.

At the window, Kinkaid looked out at the colony the humans had put up on Alba. Around it was a high wall. On top of the wall were many guns.

Lor'l joined Kinkaid at the window. "I see no Albans out there."

Kinkaid said, "No, but when we go out there —be careful, Lor'l."

He went to the door of the ship. Before he opened it, he said to his crew, "Get your laser guns." He held his own in his hand.

When Karen, Zeno, and Lor'l were armed, Kinkaid opened the door. He climbed down the steps to the blue ground.

Behind him came the others. Karen looked from side to side. Zeno pointed his gun at nothing.

"OK," Kinkaid said. "Let's move fast now. Head for the door in the wall over there."

They had gone only a little way when a flash of laser light came from behind and went over their heads.

Zeno turned and fired. But there was no one to be seen. A second flash of laser light shot past them.

"The shots came from those hills," Lor'l said to Kinkaid.

"I know. Face the hills. Back up toward the wall."

They moved on. They had almost reached the wall when they saw the Albans. They came running toward them from the hills.

"Animals," Karen said, and fired at them.

Zeno's mouth opened to show his sharp teeth. He also fired at the Albans.

But they kept coming. They were tall—over nine feet tall. And very thin. Their skin was the color of gold. On each of their heads was a gold horn. And as they ran, they sang. But their song had no words, only sounds. To Kinkaid, the song sounded like screams.

Kinkaid fired, and an Alban hit the ground. Zeno hit one too.

Karen let out a cry. She was hit. Her leg was covered with blood.

"Zeno!" Kinkaid yelled. "Help her."

But Zeno didn't seem to hear Kinkaid. He kept firing at the Albans as he backed toward the wall.

Kinkaid made his way toward Karen. She was closer to the wall than he was. But he couldn't get to her. The fire from the Albans' lasers kept him away from her.

Lor'l had almost reached the wall when Karen fell. He ran back toward her. Karen saw him coming.

When he reached her, Lor'l tried to lift her. But she pushed him in front of her. Because of her push, Lor'l found himself between her and the Albans. He stood his ground. He fired several times at the Albans.

Karen pulled herself along the ground. She moved toward the wall.

"Use your gun!" Kinkaid yelled at her.

But she didn't. Instead, she let it drop from her hand. She kept her eyes on the door in the wall.

Kinkaid, firing, moved toward Lor'l. He had

almost reached him when he heard Lor'l
scream. He saw his friend fall.

"*Lor'l!*" he yelled.

Laser lights of many colors flashed around
Kinkaid. He didn't care. He had to get to
Lor'l. The song of the Albans—those screaming
sounds—was all he could hear.

He finally reached Lor'l. "Get up!" he said. It
was an order. But Lor'l couldn't do anything
about it.

His great eye closed.

Kinkaid picked up the body of his friend.
Then he backed toward the wall, firing all the

way. When he reached the wall, Karen was already there. She was trying to open the door.

Zeno joined them. "These Albans don't stop!" he yelled. "There must be hundreds of them!"

Kinkaid put Lor'l down on the ground. Then he tried the door.

Locked!

He pounded on the door. Suddenly, there were several humans on top of the wall. When they saw what was happening, they fired at the Albans.

The Albans fell back. The people on top of the wall killed several of them. The rest ran away.

A few minutes later, the song of the Albans couldn't be heard. No laser lights flashed. The people climbed down from the wall. They opened the door.

"Why didn't you come sooner?" Kinkaid yelled at them.

"We were busy," they said.

With an angry look at them, Kinkaid picked up Lor'l. He carried him into the colony. Zeno helped Karen into the colony.

"Lor'l," Kinkaid whispered after he had

placed his friend on the ground again. "Lor'l."

Lor'l didn't move. But his eye opened. "Kinkaid, is it you?"

"It's me."

"I hurt," Lor'l said.

"You'll be OK," Kinkaid said. It was a lie. And he knew it.

Lor'l's head turned from side to side. "No," he said. "I will die."

Kinkaid looked down at the torn fur on Lor'l's body. At the holes burned in his body by the laser lights.

"I'll get help," he said. He started to get up.

Lor'l reached up. He grabbed Kinkaid's arms. "Don't go. Nothing can help me now. It's too late. Don't leave me."

Kinkaid stayed. Lor'l held his arm and looked up at the sky. A red sun burned hot.

"That sun is not like the one on my home planet," Lor'l said. "Ours is green. Our two moons are also green. I thought—I hoped—I would see my sun and moons again. Them—and my family. But it is not to be."

Kinkaid couldn't speak.

Lor'l tried to smile, but he couldn't. "We were good friends, Kinkaid," he said. "My life has been better because I knew you. Now. . . ."

He let go of Kinkaid's arm. His great eye closed. He said something. One word.

Kinkaid heard it. The word was "good-bye."

Kinkaid's head dropped into his hands. For several minutes he didn't move. Then he got to his feet. He looked down at Karen, who lay on the ground.

"I saw what you did," he said.

"What are you talking about, Kinkaid?"

"You pushed Lor'l in front of you out there."

"I didn't!"

"You did. I saw you do it. Lor'l is dead because of what you did."

"He was only an *alien*!" Karen screamed at Kinkaid. "I'm *human*!"

Kinkaid took a step toward her. He was so angry he wanted to hit something. He stood there, looking down at her. Then he turned away.

He turned to the people from the colony. "You said you didn't help us right away because you were busy. What were you doing?"

"It was time to take our Printh," one man said.

Printh!

Kinkaid knew about the drug. It put those who took it to sleep. It gave them wild dreams.

"Help her," he ordered the people. They lifted Karen into their arms.

Kinkaid went to the nearest building. He looked inside it. A woman inside the building was sleeping. There was a smile on her face. On a table near her bed was a white bag full of Printh.

Kinkaid left the building and went back to Lor'l. He looked down at his friend. He said some words. The words he said to himself were hard and ugly ones. He said them several times. But they didn't help Lor'l. They didn't help Kinkaid, either.

CHAPTER **5**

NO GOLD, NO LIFE

Kinkaid had a lot of questions to ask the humans on Alba.

The people of the colony answered his questions. They said they always spent part of each day taking Printh. Always at the same time. Yes, they said, someone should have been up on the wall when the Albans came. The person who should have been there would get in trouble. No, it wouldn't happen again.

In answer to Kinkaid's question about Alison, they said that the Albans had her in the hills. The Albans had a fort there. The people told him where it was.

Kinkaid asked why the Albans and the humans were not friends.

"Because of the gold," he was told.

What did the people mean? What was this about gold?

They told him that there was a lot of gold on Alba. They dug it out of the mines, they said. Then they sent it where Adam Lane told them to send it. He paid them for it—with money and Printh.

"But the Albans don't want you to take their gold, is that it?" Kinkaid asked.

"That's it," the people said. They added that they paid the Albans for the gold out of the money Lane gave them for it.

"But it's their gold," Kinkaid said. "The Albans should get *all* the money for it."

The people didn't think they should, and they said so. They said that they themselves dug the gold out of the mines. So they thought they should get paid for it.

Next day, Kinkaid walked through the colony. He didn't want to be with Karen or Zeno. He wanted to be by himself.

He stopped at the building where the people kept the Alban gold. He looked at the gold for a minute. Then he walked on.

He heard a noise. He looked around. But he couldn't tell where the noise came from. And *what* was the noise? He had never heard one like it before.

He walked to the left. He couldn't hear the noise. He turned back. It was louder. He decided the noise was coming from behind the building near him. He went around the side of the building. At first, he didn't see anything. He stood there, listening to the sound.

Zip-zing. Zip-zing-a-zing. Zing.

Something moved behind him. He reached for his gun and turned.

At his feet lay an Alban.

Kinkaid looked down at the Alban. Then he put his gun away. He got down on the ground beside the Alban.

The Alban's thin, gold body didn't shine. The alien tried to move. But he couldn't.

"*Zip-zing,*" he said.

"I'm a human," Kinkaid said to the alien. "I can't understand you."

"A human," said the alien. It looked up at Kinkaid, and then it closed its eyes.

"What's the matter with you?" Kinkaid asked.

At first, he got no answer. But then the alien opened his eyes. "No gold," he said.

"But I was told there's a lot of gold in the mines here."

"The humans take it all," the alien said. "Without it, all the Albans will die. No children will be born to us. Soon this star will know us no more."

"What do you mean?"

The Alban explained that he and his people needed the gold in order to live. Just as humans needed iron in their blood, Albans needed gold in theirs. But, the alien went on, the humans were taking all the gold from the mines. Soon it would all be gone.

"I came here to steal some gold," the alien said in a weak voice. "I climbed over the wall when no one was looking. I need gold. I am very sick."

"I understand everything now," Kinkaid said. "That's why you Albans are trying to drive the humans from your star, isn't it? So you can keep the gold you need to live."

"That is true," the alien said. And then, "*Zip-zip-zing.*"

"What's wrong?" Kinkaid asked.

The alien didn't answer him. He kept on making strange sounds. Then, all at once, he began to turn black. In another minute he was dead.

Kinkaid stood up. "That sound," he said to himself. "That must have been the Alban's death song."

He walked away. So, he thought, Lane had not told him everything about Alba. Or about what Lane was doing here.

But, he thought, that's Lane's business. Mine is to get his daughter away from the Albans. That's all. Nothing more.

But he couldn't forget the dead Alban or what he had said. He returned to the building where he was staying. He found Karen and Zeno inside it.

He told them nothing about what had just

happened. He asked Karen how her bad leg was.

"Better," she said.

"Can you walk now?"

She said she could.

"Good," Kinkaid said. "Because we have to go up into the hills. We have to find the Alban fort and free Alison Lane."

He told them what he thought they should do.

"Go on foot?" Zeno said when he finished. "Why not take our ship? Then we could blow up the fort."

Kinkaid said, "And kill Alison, too? That's a really great plan, Zeno. Really great."

Karen said, "A dead daughter is not what Lane wants."

"I don't care what Lane wants!" Zeno yelled. "We should take his ship and get out of here. We should have done it before. We *can* do it now."

"Sure you can," Kinkaid said. "I could stop you. But I won't. It's up to you two to decide if you're coming with me or not."

"I'm coming with you," Karen said.

"Zeno?" Kinkaid said.

"OK, OK. I'm in. When do we start?"

"Right now," Kinkaid said. "Get your lasers. Bring some food. We may be gone for a long time."

"We may be dead in a short time," Zeno said. But he got his gun.

Karen brought some food. Kinkaid got some rope and a strong iron hook.

The three of them left the building and then the colony.

"This way," Kinkaid said, and pointed. "Now let's move!"

CHAPTER **6**
ALISON

It was dark when they reached the Alban fort. Kinkaid was the first to spot it. "There it is," he said.

"What now?" Zeno asked.

"We go in," was Kinkaid's answer.

"How?" Karen asked.

Instead of answering her, Kinkaid began to move toward the fort. Like a cat, he walked without making a sound. When he reached the wall of the fort, he took the iron hook and tied it to one end of the rope. Then he threw the hook up to the top of the wall. The hook didn't catch. It fell back down. He tried a second time. The same thing. The third time the hook caught. He pulled on it. It held.

He waved to Karen and Zeno. They joined him at the wall.

"I'll climb up first," Kinkaid said. "Once I'm

on top of the wall, you climb the rope, Karen.
Then you, Zeno."

Kinkaid grabbed the rope. He climbed up it,
hand over hand. Soon he was on top of the wall.

Karen began to climb. She got to the top.
Then Zeno climbed up to join them.

"Now we have a problem," Kinkaid said.

"What's the problem?" Karen asked.

"Where do we find Alison Lane?" Kinkaid
answered.

He looked down at the buildings inside the
fort. They all looked pretty much the same. He
pulled the rope up and then dropped it down on
the inside of the fort's wall. He climbed down the
rope to the ground. Karen and Zeno climbed
down after him.

Kinkaid, still moving like a cat, went to the
nearest building. He looked in a window. At
first, he couldn't see anything. Then he made
out the shapes of several sleeping Albans.

Alison wasn't in the building. She wasn't in
the next building either. Kinkaid finally found
her in the third building he came to. She was
sleeping. There was no one with her.

"Stay here by the door," he told Karen and

Zeno. "If anyone comes—use your guns. I'll go in and get Alison."

He went into the building. He crossed the room to the bed where Alison lay. He spoke her name in a soft voice. She didn't wake up. So he reached out and touched her face.

Her eyes opened. So did her mouth.

Kinkaid put his hand over it. "Don't make any noise," he told her. "Your father sent me to get you. I'm a friend."

Alison watched his face. Kinkaid took his hand away from her mouth. He said, "Come on."

Alison didn't get up.

"*Come on!*" Kinkaid said. "We have to get away before the Albans find out I'm here."

She got up. Kinkaid went to the door and then outside. Alison came out behind him. Then she let out a loud yell.

Kinkaid tried to cover her mouth with his hand. But she got away from him. She gave another loud yell.

"*Stop that!*" Kinkaid ordered her. "You'll wake the Albans. We'll never get out of—"

Several Albans ran out of the building next

door. When they saw Kinkaid, they stopped. They pulled their laser guns. One of them threw a laser to Alison. She caught it and pointed it at Kinkaid.

Karen knocked the gun from her hand. At the same time, Kinkaid grabbed Alison and held on to her. He tried to pull her away. She put up a fight.

The Albans didn't move or fire their lasers.

Kinkaid didn't know what was happening. "Why did they throw you a gun?" he asked Alison. "I thought they had kidnapped you."

"They did kidnap me," Alison said. "But now I'm on their side."

Kinkaid wanted to ask her why she was on the Albans' side. But he didn't. There would be time for questions later—maybe. Now all he wanted to do was get out of the Alban fort and back to the colony with Alison Lane.

He started for the door in the fort's wall. Karen and Zeno joined him. All their guns were pointed at the Albans.

None of the Albans moved.

"Why don't they shoot at us?" Karen whispered to Kinkaid.

"My guess is that they don't want to hurt Alison."

Zeno raced to the door and opened it. "Let's get out of here!"

Kinkaid went through the door with Alison. Karen also went through.

Then Alison broke free of Kinkaid. She ran back toward the Albans.

But Karen reached out and grabbed her. She pulled her back through the door.

"Good work, Karen!" Kinkaid said. "Now let's get back to the colony. I don't think the Albans will give us any trouble. Not as long as we have Alison."

They headed for the colony.

An hour later, they stopped for a rest.

"Man," Zeno said, "I sweat!"

Karen opened the bag of food she had brought. She gave some to Zeno and Kinkaid. Alison wouldn't take any.

As he ate, Kinkaid watched Alison. He wondered what it was with her. First she gets herself kidnapped. Then she joins the aliens who kidnapped her.

"Alison," he said, "I told you that your father sent me here to get you away from the Albans. He's at Moon Base Two waiting for you."

"My father," Alison said. She made the word "father" sound dirty.

"He wants you back," Kinkaid. "He must love you very much."

"He does love me," Alison said. "But he loves gold more."

Kinkaid suddenly thought of the alien who had died in the colony. He asked Alison a question. "Does your father know that the Albans must have gold to live?"

"Yes," Alison said, "he knows that. After they kidnapped me, they let me talk to him. They had told me about their need for gold. I asked him if he knew about it. He said he did. He also said he was in business to make money. And that the Alban gold would bring him a lot of money."

In his mind, Kinkaid heard the sound of the Alban's death song. He said, "I think I understand what happened at that point. That's when you decided to fight with the Albans. You wanted to try to save them."

"*Do* you understand?" Alison asked him. "I've never met a human yet who cares what happens to the Albans. All any of them care about is getting their hands on the Albans' gold."

"Let's cut out all the talk," Karen said. "Let's move on."

Zeno stood up. He started to walk past

Alison. She put out her foot and tripped him.

Zeno fell. His gun flew from his hand. Alison grabbed the gun and pointed it at Kinkaid.

Karen reached for her gun.

Alison turned on her. "I may not be a very good shot," she said. "But I'm fast. So don't try anything."

Kinkaid didn't move. He looked at Alison's face. And then at the laser in her hand. "What now?" he asked her.

"I don't want to kill any of you. So don't move." She began to back away.

"We have to do something, Kinkaid," Zeno whispered. "We can't let her get away. Without her, we lose this little game of ours. Lane won't help us stay free if we don't give him his daughter."

Kinkaid still didn't move. Thoughts raced through his mind. When Zeno saw that Kinkaid wasn't moving, he acted. He made a grab for Alison.

She fired at him. He jumped back and bumped into Karen. Both of them fell down. Alison turned and ran. In less than a minute, she was out of sight.

"Let her go," Karen said.

"But we need her!" Zeno said.

"Would you rather have *her*—or all that gold back in the colony?"

Zeno looked at Karen. He began to smile. Then his smile was gone. "But Lane said he would have his men hunt us down if we just run."

"And that they would kill us when they found us," Karen said.

"Right," Zeno said. "That's what he said."

"But they won't," Karen said. "Not if we kill them first. And that's *if* they find us at all."

"That gold will go a long way for the three of us," Zeno said.

"For the *two* of us," Karen said and pointed her gun at Kinkaid. "It's going to be just you and me from now on, Zeno."

Zeno pushed Karen's gun to the side. "Let me," he said. To Kinkaid he said, "I told you that you would pay for what you did to me on the ship."

He fired.

CHAPTER 7

WAR SONG

Kinkaid ducked.

Zeno's shot went over his head. He didn't wait for Zeno to fire a second time. He raced forward, grabbed his hand, and forced the gun from it.

Karen jumped him. But Kinkaid threw her from his back. She ran. Zeno ran after her.

Kinkaid turned and set out after Alison.

As he ran through the dark, he thought about the prison planet. But there were no wild dogs after him now. The wild dogs named Karen and Zeno had gone the other way.

He finally caught up with Alison.

"Don't come any closer," she told him. She held her gun on him.

Kinkaid spoke to her. "Your father didn't tell me about the gold. I didn't know how much the Albans needed it. I just learned that a little while ago—a dying Alban told me."

"Who are you?" Alison asked. "Where are you from?"

"My name is Brett Kinkaid. I'm from. . . ." Kinkaid didn't want to tell her where he was from. But he did. "I'm from Earth."

"The prison planet?" Alison took a step away from him. Then another.

"Let me explain," Kinkaid said. He told her how he had come to be on the prison planet.

Alison said, "You say you killed the man in self-defense. Is that really true?"

"It is."

"Why are you after me now?"

"I came after you because I want to help the Albans."

"You didn't want to help them before."

"I—before, I thought I just had one job to do: get you back to your father. But I've thought things over since then. I've changed my mind."

"I don't believe you," Alison said.

"Look, I could have stopped you from getting away back there. I didn't. I let you get away because I had made up my mind to join you."

Alison didn't say anything for a minute. Then she said, "Come on. We can make the fort in a short time. But if you try anything funny. . . ." She waved the gun at Kinkaid.

He held up his hands. And smiled.

Alison didn't smile.

When they reached the fort, Alison took Kinkaid to the leader of the Albans. She told him what Kinkaid wanted to do.

"Can we believe what he says?" the leader asked her.

"Yes," Alison said. She looked at Kinkaid. Her look seemed to ask him if what she had just said was really true.

Kinkaid said, "I think we can take the colony. We can stop the people from working your gold mines."

The leader of the Albans looked down. "There are not many of us left now. The humans have killed great numbers of our brothers and sisters. Some of us have died because we have no gold."

"We can still do it," Kinkaid said. "Let me tell you my plan."

After he had told them, everyone got ready to go to the colony.

Kinkaid led the way. Alison walked beside him. Behind them came the Albans. The Albans began to sing their war song.

It was the song Kinkaid had heard before. That time he didn't like it. But now he thought it sounded just fine. He even joined in the singing once he learned the sounds.

"They'll hear us coming," Alison said.

Kinkaid shook his head. "No, they won't. This is the time of day when they always take their Printh. The drug will keep them from hearing us."

But Kinkaid was wrong. Two of the people in the colony were not sleeping. Two men stood on top of the colony's wall. When they saw the Albans, they began to shoot.

Kinkaid ran through their fire toward the wall. In his hands was the rope he had used to climb into the Alban fort. He threw an end of it at one of the men. The rope went around the man's neck. Kinkaid pulled hard. The man was off balance. He fell from the wall. The Albans caught and held him. Then Kinkaid drew his laser gun and blasted the other man.

He threw his rope a second time. This time it caught on top of the wall. He climbed up the rope. Then he climbed down inside the colony.

He opened up the door in the wall from the inside.

As the Albans came into the colony, he gave them orders. They went into all the buildings. They woke the people from their drugged sleep.

They brought them outside and made them all stand together.

Kinkaid looked at the group of people. Karen wasn't in the group. Zeno wasn't either.

He asked himself if he was too late. He ran to the building where the people kept the Alban gold. It was empty. He ran from the colony toward the spaceship.

When he got to the ship, he climbed on board. Inside the ship was the gold. It was piled up on the floor.

Karen was on board. She spotted Kinkaid. She yelled for Zeno. Zeno came running. Both of them went after Kinkaid.

But he dropped Zeno as he had once dropped the dog Cyclops. And he knocked Karen's laser from her hand before she could get off a shot.

Then he made the two of them leave the ship. He took them back to the colony. Once there, he made them join the group of people the Albans were watching over. Then Kinkaid went back to his ship.

He stood before its control board. There was one last thing he had to do. He looked down at the orange button on the control board. He had come to press it. But when he did press it, everything would be all over for him.

He pressed the button and called the Space Police.

"Space Police here," a voice said.

"Come to the star Alba," Kinkaid said. "I have a group of humans here. They are murderers." He explained that the people had been taking the Albans' gold.

"That doesn't make them murderers," the voice said.

"Oh, yes, it does," Kinkaid said. He explained that the Albans needed gold just as humans needed iron in their blood. Without the gold, he said, the Albans would die.

"So you see," he said, "the humans are killing

the Albans by taking their gold. That makes them murderers."

"Who are you?" the voice asked.

Kinkaid had been waiting for that question. He thought of not answering. Of flying the ship away and. . . .

He said, "My name is Brett Kinkaid."

"*Kinkaid!*" the voice said. "We've been looking for you for a long time—ever since you escaped from the prison planet. Stay right where you are. We're on our way."

Kinkaid wondered how the police knew he had escaped from Earth. Well, it didn't matter. They knew. That was the important thing.

He left the ship and returned to the colony.

He told Alison what he had just done.

"But they'll take you back to Earth!" she said. "You'll never get away again. And it was my father who got you into this!"

Kinkaid didn't say anything. There was really nothing to say. They waited quietly for the Space Police to come.

It wasn't long before two Space Police ships flew over their heads. One of them was a big prison ship. Both of them landed.

The police left their ships and came into the colony. They put all the colony people and

Karen and Zeno on board the prison ship. Just before Karen got on board, she looked back at Kinkaid. Her eyes flashed. Zeno didn't look back.

The commander of the police came over to Kinkaid. "How did you escape from the prison planet, Kinkaid?"

Kinkaid told him about Adam Lane. "He set up this deal to mine the Alban gold."

"Then he'll have to stand trial for murder, too," the commander said. "Just as those people of his will. Do you know where he is now, Kinkaid?"

Kinkaid looked at Alison.

She looked down at the ground. "Tell him, Kinkaid," she said.

"You'll find Adam Lane on Moon Base Two. I was supposed to meet him there."

"We'll go there and get him," the commander said.

Kinkaid said, "I'm ready to go back to Earth."

"No, you're not," the commander said. "I was just about to tell you—"

"Tell me what?"

"Do you remember the man in your old command who spoke against you at your trial?"

"I'll never forget him," Kinkaid said. What, he wondered, was this all about?

"He died," the commander said. "But just before he died, he called us. He told us he had lied—that he had set you up."

"That's what I said at my trial!" Kinkaid said. "But no one would believe me!"

"They believe you now, Kinkaid. So you're a free man. We went to Earth to tell you that. That's how we knew you had escaped. Oh, one more thing. Your old command is yours again —if you want it."

"I want it," Kinkaid said in a soft voice. "I want it very much."

The commander said, "You have it." Then he left. The two ships flew into the sky.

Kinkaid and Alison went to Kinkaid's ship. They took the gold from it and gave it back to the Albans. Then Kinkaid got the ship ready to leave Alba. "What are you going to do, Alison?"

"I don't know," she said. "But I do know I have to start my life all over again."

"So do I," Kinkaid said. And he added, "As Commander Kinkaid of the Space Police."

"Is it a good life?" Alison asked.

"The best," he answered.